ANTHOLOGY 2021

Beaten Track
www.beatentrackpublishing.com

Literary Lancashire Award Anthology 2021

First published 2021 by Beaten Track Publishing
Copyright © 2021 Literary Lancashire Award
Edited by Amy Cavanagh

Paperback: 978 1 78645 509 3
Hardcover: 978 1 78645 510 9
eBook: 978 1 78645 511 6

Cover Design: Alix Leonard

Beaten Track Publishing,
Burscough, Lancashire.
www.beatentrackpublishing.com

Thanks to the English Literature and Creative Writing Department at Lancaster University, whose ongoing support throughout our project has provided us with much guidance, and whose financial donation has enabled this project to truly accomplish its goals.

Thanks to our Poetry and Prose judges, who volunteered their time to the difficult task of shortlisting our many excellent entries and provided us with wonderful feedback.

Thanks to our judges, Drs Zoe Lambert and Eoghan Walls for donating their expertise in creative writing to select this year's winners and runners-up.

A big thank-you to all the entrants who submitted this year. We had tons of fantastic submissions, which our judging team thoroughly enjoyed reading.

And, finally, thanks to our very generous supporters on our GoFundMe page—this wouldn't be possible without you.

CONTENTS

FOREWORD

The Literary Lancashire Award was founded in 2019 by Ruth Walbank and Lara Oriss and is now in its third year of running.

The award is designed to be an opportunity for young writers in Lancashire to experiment with creativity whilst simultaneously taking that first step into building an impressive portfolio.

This year's entries were extremely fun to read, and our team has been eagerly anticipating the publication of *The Literary Lancashire Award Anthology 2021.*

Our team has worked tirelessly since October 2020, so a big thank-you to our wonderful team members:

Millie Holden, Online Content Officer

Ellen Darbyshire, Online Content Officer

Khatijah Balu, Funding Officer

Sravudh Tanhai, Admin Officer

Daniel Findell, Co-Head Organiser,
Judging and Recruitment

Amy Cavanagh, Co-Head Organiser,
Finance and Marketing

We hope you have as much fun exploring the creativity of Lancashire's writers as we did.

OUR THEMES

Each year, we set several themes for entries to be submitted under. We find these themes can be a useful way to get ideas flowing, as we keep them open and broad in their interpretation. This year's themes are:

- A Glimpse of Familiarity

- Locked Away

- A Shift in Time

- Out of Control

- The Creature

'Loss isn't an absence after all. It is a presence.'
– Jackie Kay, *Trumpet*

'...to me life had lost its relish when liberty was gone.'
– Olaudah Equiano, *The Interesting Narrative of the Life of Olaudah Equiano*

SHORT FORM POETRY CONTEST

WINNERS

X+Y

by Sam Allport

Friendship is terrible. It leaves you head-spun,
Half-chewed, tossed off-axis and
Talking in axis tongues.
You and I and I and you
Are fused in each other's minds, chainmail
Hula hoops, Olympic rings. Our Gordian knot
Is stretched taut
But we cling.
I cling.

WAIL AT THE FOOT OF LIA FAIL

by Beth Train-Brown

i kissed a sìdhe
in a circle of mushrooms
next to the house
in the middle of the M6

(he tasted like beer)
(he tasted like an open fire)

i taught him latin
and watched him cry
watched him palm the tears
and swallow them

(i bit the Blarney Stone)

THE MOUTH OF HEAVEN

by Alex Roman

The friction of the putrid machine
scorches the surface of this world,
laminating it in polyethylene,
as all life furled

Blood drips from our wallets,
earned through gritted moans,
all to build these whatchamacallits,
packed like sardines with human bones

PROSE

WINNER

PANDO
BY KATIE KINGSMAN

'I loved the ambition of this story in both its use of point of view and its structure, oscillating between different time periods, sometimes millions and thousands of years apart. The story is revealed to be voiced by the 'Pando' itself. There was extensive research used to write this story, but this was so deftly included, and couples with a lovely use of imagery and detail.'

– Zoe Lambert
Head Prose Judge

PANDO

by Katie Kingsman

1980 AD.

I used to be Sisyphean.

I am not recollection, or memory.

I am the last of the vagabond.

Seven Million Years Ago.

On the Saharan planes, alone amid the dust and dried-out yellow grass, an early human leans back, stretches, and walks on two legs for the first time.

1972 AD.

I've heard the names, dropped from tourists with waterproof hiking boots (PAN.DO). They walk across the terrain. Carefully constructed ergonomic soles pinch at my exposed roots, eroding away at the fine soil I rest in. (Forty-three hectares).

200,0000 BC.

For many generations, it existed as a myth, an incomprehensible mirage creeping in from the edge of the world. Tectonic plates still moved beneath the surface like disrupted algae. Seeds sprouted, and the sand solidified into land. All the time, it crept across the ocean until it crested the horizon of a curious group of humans. The rest of the world unfolded itself.

1968 AD.

Org-an-ism.

80,000 BC.

The wild still rules the world. Storms rear waves through the sky as if a megalodon still ghosts its territory. People run from beasts with claws and fangs. In a land still void of humans, a seed of quaking aspen takes root.

Neither knows how big they'll become.

1790 AD.

Urbanisation, materialisation.

(The Wilderness Tamed)

64,000 BC.

A Neanderthal sees the shape and pattern the days take and starts to wonder. The way the wolves move makes him feel something strange, something more than fear. He looks at the setting sun, the breath of a bison, the cloud of hot mist that rises above the herd on a cold morning.

Something compels him to capture it on the walls of a cave.

A red stencil to outlast the ice ages and species that made it. Until the cave it resides in comes to be known as Maltravieso in Caceres, Spain. It is the oldest known surviving cave painting, and the earliest evidence of art.

1492 AD.

They smelt like smoke. Salt and burning and rot.
I was centred on a wood pigeon, sunken in my arms
as it took its last few breaths, but with the step that
unloosed earth, my entire being shivered.

2611 BC.

Pharaoh Khufu stands in the shadow of the Great Pyramid of Giza. The sand at his feet has been kept from the sun for hours now, and despite the prickling wind that pulls the sweat from his veins, the ground remains cold in the wake of his vision.

His tomb reaches to the sky. The wind's course is cracked by the monument's weight. Around Khufu and his legacy, the sands still shimmer and migrate. But not here, where Khufu stands the wind, and the sun cannot reach.

2,227 BC.

More People come. Eventually, people die.

They put their bodies in the ground. To me.

They return my old branches, marred with whorls and horsehair. Chipped, oiled, loved. Arms to arms.

600 BC.

Enlightenment. Before this moment, he must have been blind. The past becomes grey, flat, prehistoric. The words push through the bones of his fingers and change the world. In the Ancient Kingdom of Magadha, Siddhartha Gautama discovers a new type of truth and Buddhism is born.

5,401 BC.

He stays in my sphere. Pulled, lulled like a satellite. Hunting elk, forging new things from my branches. The closed-cup mushrooms and dark, blue berries make him smile.

The world takes on a vibrant edge. Still—

I house, I feed, I grow.

1.AD.

The world fractures again. An old religion is divided and reconceptualised. Christ is born.

9,020 BC.

Yes, it hurt. Naturally, the way a bear sharpening its claws to bring out sap would sting. Or a family of woodworm gorging would itch.

But, I am more than just one vessel.

500 AD.

They called it the Dark Ages.

12,308 BC.

The branch of a tree snaps away in a hunter's grip.

That fragment of me, the tree by the river, grew for a few thousand more years. One of many that lick of the woods. They/I grew to shadow the crest of a valley that flooded with every spring-melt.

Generationally, a family of hawfinches would nest in the groove left from the hunter's knife.

If the woods could talk.

905 AD.

A powder invented by the Taoists to cure human ailments is bastardised. For the first time it is used for mechanical warfare. It is the perfection of gunpowder.

21,641 BC.

Learn. Recede. Conquer.

I climb the rocky barren mountains and relinquish acidic earth.

I am used to change and all of this that comes. All takes time. There's cycles and seasons and juddering, earthly rotations noticed only in the touch of wind and the patterns in the sky.

Nothing can stop me.

(Conkers)

1503 AD.

Da Vinci finishes work on the *Mona Lisa*.

40,100 BC.

If a tree falls? (Which tree) If a tree falls in a forest and nobody sees, does it really fall? (What about an eyelash? Do you notice when a skin cell dies?)

1610 AD.

In the heart of an unnamed woods.

I get the sense of something long dead, or something that should have died a long time ago that lingers still.

The branches hang terribly in the coming night.

I can sense something sinister in the way the branches move above me. I am watching them now. Each leaf is identical. Some leaves fall from their branches and hit the ground at the same time.

53,900 BC.

Storms and seasons. They indent themselves as a dark mark hidden in my cracked bark. Etched like a ripple from a stone in the water. Creating its own chronicle, erupting through my own growth marks.

For lightning, we are the path of least resistance. The easiest way to express substance and escape from the. Unfortunately:

Lightning damage is instantaneous.

1790 AD.

The birth of industrialisation and the beginning of manmade climate change.

66,020 BC.

In the Beginning, there was a mighty Oak;

An unbelievable age, and unbelievable size!
I thought, until my roots touched theirs.

Weak to disease, weak to drought and starvation.
Such a small system could never survive.

Not without me.

Certainly not with me.

Underneath the leaf litter, it recoiled, trapped by
its trunk as thick as a boulder. Too big, too singular,
nothing to sustain.

What a short history.

All I did was wait; grow and wait.

1899 AD.

Hitler is born.

72,000 BC.

(That way).

In the south, near the sea, my leaves begin
to bud.

1903 AD.

Humans claim the sky. Marked by a stuttering wake of grey fumes, people fly.

80,000 BC.

In the age of Glaciers, a seed falls into rich, wet spring soil.

Across the oceans and not for the first time, an almost-bipedal animal picks up a sharpened stone and runs from a Smilodon, foaming at the mouth.

1912 AD.

The entire world shivers on the brink of war. In the middle of the ocean, among severed icebergs, the *Titanic*, a testament to man's industrial power, succumbs to the freezing waves.

67,300 BC.

(Spring)

Sap. Tandem. Coded copied.

I untangle the steadings of a grove of Whit Ash. Gradually, I push their system out of the earth. Uprooted, I seep further into the valley.

1967 AD.

A man is given a second chance at life. They crack his ribs open, and one man's heart is replaced with another's. Foreign tissue basted in blood. Washkansky's rebirth of eighteen days.

53,400 BC.

(About a mile from Fish Lake, Utah)

A long time before, I lived along the banks of the marshlands and the quarries as I do now. The soil was rich for a time, and the animals grew big and peaceful. The earth was warmed, the animals left, and...

I receded too.

Now, I return again. My roots embrace the ground like an old friend. Mammoths follow me. A dictated migration.

They were the biggest annoyance, with a habit to eat spring leaves as fast as I could produce them. Solution? I grew taller, until those nosey beasts could not reach. They were big but—

I am monolithic.

1968 AD.

The botanist Burton Barnes suspects something strange about the grove of quaking aspens he lives by. He discovers the biggest ever known organism and names It:

Pando.

47,000 BC.

Springtime is cooler than usual. Migrating bison shuffle through.

Blundering forms ricochet and scrape against me. The infant saplings split and turn to cud against blunt teeth.

Some of the bison with saggy skin and ailing bones cannot withstand the boreal air.

I welcome them into the ground.

2005 AD.

A man sits at his kitchen table in his desert home, with two broken legs and his son and grandson upstairs. He calls his much younger wife at the gym, says goodbye. Loads his pistol and blows his brains out.

32,900 BC.

I grow well. Balloon up under the unrelenting sun to spill out into the world and beyond. I spread like clouds blown in the wind. Not until late autumn do my leaves begin to fall.

2012 AD.

The doctor explains the process of an eye ultrasound, smearing cold jelly across an eye.

"Stay still now—no-ah, no, don't lean back."

Feet get callouses from walking. Gums bleed and skin turns cancerous. The body brunts the pain.

7,030 BC.

I soak up the carbon from their jaws. It drips out on the frosted air.

Their lives carry just one of my lungfuls.

I cradle them in my roots, careful.

(Grip).

Bodies can bubble under the mulch; I soak it up.

2020 AD.

The modern human world wrenches to a standstill. The culprit: pulmonary disease.

Unequipped to battle a pandemic, people are placed under a global lockdown. Countless die.

A jellyfish swims through the crystal-clear canals of Venice. The city still stinks.

890 AD.

A rudimentary city finds itself underneath my branches. I find myself poking up between holes in the manmade rocks.

Something is leeching into the ground.

Things with no roots. Bark without soul and bodies without blood vessels. In my centre, where the first root took hold, they fight the fiercest.

Light splits through the sky like a wolf's howl.

2049 AD.

Russia creates an artificial landmass out of deposited sand off the coast of Poland.

1790 AD.

A machine designed to spin wool becomes popular. Fabric hairs line the air.

Sallow ground.

We used to co-exist, now they.   Fester.

The people's air turns ugly. Venomous smoke; the colour of a vicious storm. Warning. The ground gets harsh.

(Grow that way.)

In my depths, the animals begin to scream.

2068 AD.

The world population figure breaks 10 billion.

2012 AD.

The world is warm and sour. I am just a pond of life now.

Escape evades me.

"...Pando is currently thought to be dying..."

My fate was sealed the moment those first leather boots stepped into the dust.

2094 AD.

Pando's leaves refuse to bud. The ground through the forest concaves as the roots turn to mulch in the earth. On a strong wind from the south at the heart of summer, the bark comes loose as dust and ashes. It lands in swathes on the oak-framed windows of Californian houses.

2040 AD.

A fire that smoulders and rots from the inside. A new type of plague or parasite. The hunter's bullet. Poison iron and heat. Bark to ashes. In the earth, my roots get twisted. I am the invisible casualty.

Though not for long.

2153 AD.

The last trunk of Pando is cut down and splintered into wood shavings. Sea levels rise to completely submerge New York, while the absence of forestry turns American terrain into the fourth most uninhabitable desert in the world.

2068 AD.

Deer and wild warthogs strip at my bark, exposing my raw skin to the blazing, new-age heat. If my new saplings can make it through the peat and prying grazers, they simmer in the sun.

My roots are stagnant. The springtime bloom feels like wading into quicksand. Leaves grow yellow with sickness, and by the summer solstice, they curl and crumble in the wind.

RUNNERS UP

EXAMINATION
BY DITTE JENSEN

'I loved how this story drew us into what seems an ordinary world, but it is revealed to be a dystopian and horrifying examination process. Brilliantly written with an electric ending.'

& THE TEMPO IS ALL MINE
BY CHARLOTTE LLOYD

'I felt so drawn into this story about two students. It was simply but richly told, and underneath the character's creativity, there is a hint of trauma. All very involving.'

– Zoe Lambert
Head Prose Judge

EXAMINATION

by Ditte Jensen

The world is still, and by the time one would expect morning to arrive, its light like honey spreading across my bedroom floor; the night still lingers. I put the kettle on even though I don't drink tea or coffee—the taste reminds me of grain at the bottom of wheat barrels, of stale sourdough—because I don't know what else to do with myself. If nothing else, its whistle will permeate the apartment and chase away the nauseating silence.

I'm taking up far too much space, my breathing too loud, my hands too restless. I am all too aware of my own presence like a sculpture in a home that holds no place.

In the living room, I uncover a knitted blanket that once belonged to my mother and wrap it around my shoulders. Her scent, rose and pungent lavender, still lingers between its threads; or perhaps it's my own. Maybe I have finally turned into my mother at the ripe age of twenty-one.

The living room walls largely consist of windowpanes, most of which face the town centre and to the east, the old national park once crowned by foliage, melting into sharp gold and emerald by the morning sunlight. The town square is illuminated by clinical streetlights; the park has been swallowed by the darkness.

The large windows used to be my favourite fixture of the apartment. When I was fresh out of business college two years ago, unfamiliar with the world, a newly hatched egg, it was Adam who'd introduced me to the landlord—a friend of his father's, willing to rent to any friend of Adam's. I'd met Adam during my senior year. He was studying biotechnology and mathematics, and he moved too fast for the world to keep up. He was always working on a million projects at once and abandoned each one as soon as his heart had moved elsewhere, to something new and unfamiliar. Still, he always devoted himself fully to every project. I asked him about it once when we were sitting on my living room floor. I was drinking cheap German white wine while watching him sift through a folder with a number of sketches he'd done of places around Copenhagen including the King's Garden with its intricate wildlife, the statues mounted on top of the Gefion Fountain and The Marble Church whose dome rose through a smattering of curtained clouds.

"I give everything I do my full attention," he said. "And when I have nothing more to give, I move on to something else. There's nothing sad about it; it's just life." Sunlight had bled through the curtains then, flooding his face, the freckles on his cheek like stars, and he kissed me.

Now, the sun never rises, and the windows are riddled with a hollow darkness that makes me hate the living room more than any other space in my apartment.

Adam shows up at my door at quarter past seven, dressed in a three-piece. I gave him a set of keys two years ago, but he still insists on knocking. "Are you ready to go?" he asks and plants a kiss on the tip of my nose. I make him wait in the kitchen with a cup of peppermint tea while I disappear into the bedroom to get dressed. As I pull the dress over my shoulders—a white summer dress with a blue silk ribbon pinned to the back—I feel a sudden jolt in my stomach and stumble into the bathroom to throw up.

I lie there for a moment, bent over the toilet bowl. Acid stings my eyes and the back of my throat. I consider staying there, if only for a moment longer.

"Alma, is everything okay?"

"I'll be just a minute," I say and pull myself up from the bathroom floor. I take another moment to secure my dress and brush my teeth, which makes my mouth burn. I find him standing in the kitchen, his back turned until he hears me enter. His eyes stumble into mine. I love seeing him blush; it's as if he has been caught trespassing on land that has always belonged to him.

"Are you ready?" he asks again, and this time, I nod and take his hand. The examination hall is a short walk from the apartment, no more than ten minutes, but the darkness, endlessly pressing forward, turns time into a phantom. Seconds bleeds into weeks, minutes into years. I'm pressed to his side because the darkness is so overwhelming, so silent that, despite the streetlights evenly spaced out along the pavement, it is like walking blindly. When we are not illuminated by their spectral glow, I can't see his face, and all I have to go on is the feeling of his body next to mine, my personal anchor.

"We'll be fine," he says, but there's an uncharacteristic uncertainty in the spaces between his words. "I'll meet you outside when we're done, okay? I've spent a few extra stamps on a bottle of wine. We'll go back to yours and celebrate." He stops then. I feel his hand tightening around my own as he pulls me in front of him. His breath curls upon my face, most of his features lost to the void. In the harsh streetlights, he looks much older than he is. "I love you," he says, and I can tell he is nervous from the way he stumbles over the o's, the vulnerability on the back of his tongue bleeding through his teeth. I can't say it back even though I want to. Instead, I kiss him and say, "We can't be late."

The building itself is concrete and towers above the rest as if searching for the light we cannot see. It's surrounded by an electric fence that is connected by a metal front gate. Apart from the governmental Christiansborg Palace, it's the only building in Copenhagen that's still visible. The rest of the city has been devoured by an endless night devoid of stars.

In the darkness, the examination building appears almost surreal, so strikingly out of place among all the black that it is impossible to miss.

We present our personal identification numbers at the gate and are escorted inside the building by three soldiers. The hallways are long and narrow. I'd imagined it to be well-lit inside, but it isn't. Our path is sparsely lit by wall sconces, the space between them so outstretched that we're periodically plunged into an almost complete darkness. Although there are supposedly others inside, it's so quiet that our footsteps echo and bounce off the walls. Metal lockers are mounted to the walls, doors with small, rectangular windows look into abandoned classrooms, washed-out posters pinned on old bulletin boards.

Adam is still holding my hand.

When we reach the hall—once a gymnasium, now deformed by identical metal desks bolted into the floor in extensive rows—I'm momentarily blinded by a white light. My eyes burn in kaleidoscopic spots, and I'm overcome with an overwhelming urge to flee. I find myself missing the dark. I want it to swallow me whole, to gnaw at me until my flesh splits open to reveal the bone underneath. I want to be concealed, unseen.

Then, the piercing white fades, and in its passing, my sight returns. We're still standing in the doorway, my hand still in Adam's. In front of us are hundreds of students, all dressed in three-pieces and white summer dresses. They're all sitting at a desk. Nobody is talking.

A soldier grabs my shoulder, and I feel Adam's hand slipping from mine. I look to him to say something, but we're pulled in separate directions before I manage to say anything at all. I'm escorted to an empty desk in the third row. The metal chair bites into my thigh where my dress has scrunched up to reveal my skin, the colour of almond milk. There's a notebook, a black ink pen and an eraser on the desk in front of me. I want to turn around to see where Adam is, but even my own breath seems intrusive in the soundless hall, and I can't make myself do it.

Another twenty minutes pass before the door to the gymnasium closes. My body is fusing with the cold bursts of air that seem to come from nowhere and everywhere all at once. I'm pressing the palms of my hands against the insides of my thighs for warmth when a woman walks onto the podium. Her image is projected against the wall behind her, her features distorted by the harsh light. Her voice echoes through the speakers, dusting the halls with an almost tangible static: "As you are aware, this exam will determine whether you are considered an essential. If you fail to prove yourself, you will be deemed expendable and dealt with accordingly. You have three hours to complete the tasks before you. You may not speak to the person next to you nor ask any questions. Once the exam has begun, you may not leave the examination hall. Cheating will not be tolerated. You may begin."

The silence is momentarily ruptured as the papers are turned. I turn my own, and in that moment, I watch as every pocket of knowledge I've learnt throughout my life slips through my fingers. I remember nothing. It isn't that I'm unprepared; I've spent the last few months relentlessly revising for the exam, traded my sleep for notes in the margins. Somehow, it still feels like I've managed to waste my time.

To pass, I need to score eleven-point-eight out of twelve. I've never scored more than eleven. I loathe exams, the power they hold like a weighted noose around my neck. I prefer tests designed for a future deadline, the process of gathering information, planning and drafting over a longer burst of time. Under pressure, I crumble—I perform well, adequately even, but not brilliantly. Not good enough.

Somewhere far away, I can hear pens scribbling, soldiers' footsteps as they patrol the hall. I hunch over my desk and try to construct answers to questions I do not understand. I don't know how much time has passed, but I realise the footsteps have stopped. When I look up, a soldier is leaning over the shoulder of a red-haired boy sitting at the desk next to mine. His hands are shaking so violently that it's a wonder he's writing anything at all. On his wrist, there's a smudge of writing.

The soldier pulls something out of his belt, and it takes me a moment to register that it's a gun. It doesn't make a sound, but the boy's head slams into the desk all the same. My back whips against the back of my chair; my breath catches in my chest. I want to scream and throw up all at once, but I find myself unable to do either. Instead, I stare at the dead boy staring back at me. I vaguely register the sounds of other heads dropping, but I can't take my eyes off the red-haired boy. Somewhere in the back, a girl is screaming.

Another head collides with metal. The screaming stops.

The soldier picks up the boy and throws him over his shoulder. I don't even realise I'm crying until I look down and notice the ink has started to bleed out on the page. The soldier walks towards the front. Others follow him shortly after, surfacing from the rows behind me, all carrying bodies over their shoulders.

I'm trying to force myself to focus when I recognise one of the bodies. I want to scream, to beg, to call his name, but air whips violently against the back of my throat, suffocating me. I can't make a sound. A soldier forces me back into my seat.

The woman's voice returns to the speakers.

"May we kindly remind you that cheating is not tolerated."

& THE TEMPO IS ALL MINE

by Charlotte Lloyd

– 1 –

Harriet has been at Cambridge for the best part of a year when she decides to take Leo up on his offer of a piano. It's the summer term; languid days are escaped in frantic nights. She's exhausted. From so many things.

(A musician's room, *even though I do English*, he'd said, on the night they first met. *I have a piano. Come back with me. Didn't you say you wanted to be a concert pianist, once?* She'd laughed, thinking it was a ploy to get her to sleep with him. A couple of weeks later, she'd discovered he wasn't lying. She became curious. Now, months later, her curiosity still lingers.)

When she arrives at his door, he doesn't respond to the first light tap of her knuckles. She tries again, and after a couple of minutes gives it a push. To her surprise, it swings open.

He's sitting on the windowsill, holding on to a copy of *Middlemarch*. It's early evening, but he has a worn-in expression about him, as opposed to worn out. When his eyes lift from the novel, he meets her gaze like he was expecting to see her. It's assured, and she feels herself begin to flush.

"Don't you care about a murderer walking in, or something?" she says, standing just inside the door. She smooths her thumb over her belt loops like a worry. "Are you one?"

"Well, no. But the point isn't..." Leo shrugs, and Harriet stops, sensing that they don't have much to say to each other. That they've never had enough in common.

"I've decided that I would like to play the piano," she announces, instead.

"Now?" One of Leo's eyebrows arch upward, but she misses it. He's turned back to *Middlemarch*.

"Well, yes."

"Okay," he replies.

A steady silence develops between them, and he doesn't move from where he's sitting in the window. Harriet notes the piano, a few paces in-between them both. For the first time in months, the pads of her fingers itch to play, so she moves towards it. She hasn't done this in almost a year. She hesitates.

"And you're—you're just going to sit there?"

The evening shadows fall over his face, and he taps a pencil against the spine of the book in his lap. His shirt is untucked over the top of his jeans.

"Yes." She takes a step towards him, wishing he would meet her gaze at least. "I don't know if I'll cry."

"That's all right."

– 2 –

Leo is not sure how much time passes between his looking away and Harriet walking over to the piano. He's only determined he's not going to stare; he's going to remain interested in one of the supposed greatest novels of the Victorian period. Through his periphery, he becomes vaguely aware of Harriet removing her jacket; Harriet sitting at the piano. For at least the first hour, that's all she does. Sit. After an hour and a half, he drifts to the kitchenette to make himself dinner.

By the second hour, he's finished eating, and his eyes are swimming from reading small print. He notices Harriet smoothing her palms over the lid of the instrument. He picks up his plate and moves to the sink.

"It's not gonna bite you," he says, as he drifts past the half-open door. Harriet stiffens, and he wonders if it was a mistake.

It's on hour three, when he's really tempted to tell her to leave, that she beings to play. To begin with, Leo hastens a guess and thinks she's quite average. Scales don't require a lot of difficulty. Later, he gets the sense that as the notes increase in pitch, she too is building herself up to something of a greater magnitude.

He reinstates himself at the window, but he doubts she notices. She moves with a simultaneous lack of precision and surplus of it. Like jazz; like rehearsed chaos. Her hair falls in her face. He notices a scar on the back of her right hand that he's never registered before. At some point, he begins to drift in and out of sleep.

When he wakes some time later, he has a crook in his spine and she's walking back from the kitchen, holding something in her right hand. The one with the scar. He frowns foggily, yawing as he sits up.

"Where'd you go?"

"Made myself a Pot Noodle."

He huffs a laugh and runs a hand over his hair. "Of course you did."

They half smile at each other.

"Listen, Harriet. It's like three a.m. You won't be offended if I go to bed, will you?"

"No," she says, and sits again.

He leaves it at that, and it's only as she's by the door that he catches her voice.

"Am I doing all right?" she asks, and he realises she needs his answer.

"I'd say so," he replies.

– 3 –

It's the next morning. Leo wakes to the sound of music sliding through the air, over his consciousness. When he sees Harriet, the first thing he notes is the way the daylight gets caught in her hair. As she realises he's walked behind her, she stops playing. Neither say anything for a moment.

"What's that? That you were just playing?" he asks.

"I wrote it." She glances up at him, uncertain. There are dark circles under her eyes, like storm clouds gathering before the rain, yet she has never seemed more alive to him.

"Can you write it down for me?"

"I don't remember it. I just made it up."

Leo examines her flushed face; feels slightly winded by the honesty in her expression.

"Can you keep going?"

"I don't know."

Leo pauses. "Try," he urges.

Harriet plays, and Leo records the best parts on his phone. He's faintly aware that she has no idea what she's creating and perhaps isn't thinking anything. He wants to give the music back to her. He imagines it: saving it to a memory stick and posting it in her college mail box. *Here's what you gave to me without your knowledge,* he'd write. *And now you deserve to have it returned to you.*

On the second iteration of it, he stops her. He sits on the edge of the piano stool and is relieved when she doesn't jolt away.

"Your hand," he says, his voice rough from sleep and from something else. "What happened?"

She stalls. Shakes her head. "You're not asking about my hand. You're asking about the scar. Those are different."

"The scar, then."

She takes a breath that rattles. Drinks in his shirt that looks like crumpled paper. She decides. "When I got into Cambridge," she says her voice far steadier than she feels, "I couldn't play. Or, at least, couldn't play how I wanted. Where the music came from was numb. I remember sitting at the piano and being so furious because I couldn't do it.

Applying here had made me forget how to be myself. Do you know how difficult it is to be constantly defined by the thing that you resent even thinking about? So." She hesitates. Now, finally, there are tears in her eyes. "So, I pulled the lid of the piano down on my hand. Three times. Hard. I passed out, and I broke my knuckles."

There's a detachment in her voice, like the memories are not hers. For a moment, Leo says nothing. Then, he reaches for her hand, and runs his thumb over the top of the lighter skin.

"How long did it take to heal?" he asks. She lets out a small laugh.

"My hand? About three weeks," she says.

There's a second half of the sentence which she doesn't want to acknowledge but that she suspects Leo knows. The sun is high enough now that it warms both of their faces. She has a nine a.m. lecture. She'll have to go to it wearing yesterday's clothes, but she doesn't particularly care.

Slow enough to let her pull away if she didn't want it, Leo lifts her hand to his mouth and grazes his lips across her skin. He hears her intake of breath but is relieved when she doesn't move.

"Don't they always say that the greatest art evolves from the greatest pain?" he says, and she half shrugs.

"I suppose. Yes."

"Then I feel like I should apologise." Her eyes flick to his, and when they meet, she wonders if his face is a reflection of her own. The warmth of his skin seeps into her palm.

"Why?" she asks.

He swallows; a muscle ticks in his jaw. "Because you play so beautifully."

TWO AND NOT ONE

by Joseph Dodds

A cross-breeze blew the plume of his breath back into his face, misting his goggles. With one fleece-lined leather glove, he wiped them clear.

Not that there was much to see. The balloon, towering fifty feet above him, obscured his view to the *Fulmar*'s prow and beyond. Seeing through the huge net that encaged it was like peering through the thickest undergrowth, the close-woven cords stretching and groaning with each sway of the canvas within.

Seeing ahead was immaterial, though. They would hit nothing up here.

Professor Sir Napier Balfour stood at the console in the stern, gripping the two bronze crank handles. With a counter- or clockwise notch of either, he could unfurl or retract the port for starboard sails and dictate how the wind guided the *Fulmar* through the sky.

At this moment, the winds were good. The prevailing gust blew from the stern to push the craft forward, creaking like a ship on the sea, and yet so far from being so. Behind him, the turbine depending from the rear thrummed. With such a good wind, he had allowed the engine to slow. The great blades swept by with a slow, sleepy stroke.

The rigging lines moaned, the balloon's gas canister roared, and breezes chased each other across the deck. But for that, it was silent. Even these sounds had no echo to answer them. Out beyond the gunwales, not even a seabird called.

Balfour knew he and his companion were the northernmost beings in the world.

He turned, scanning the view. He remembered an expedition in Siberia when the sun had blazed, unfiltered, onto the snow. The effect was like crossing a mirror while a light glared off it. It withered the eyes and made the ears ring.

It was almost the same up here. The fields and plateaus of white clouds were a prism for the sun's dazzling rays. He was thankful for the tinted goggles.

He checked his watch, which was nestled up the sleeve of his hide-and-fur anorak to prevent the glass from freezing. He had been steering for an hour.

"Take the helm," he said. The air smothered his voice. Speaking in pitch silence like this made him feel somehow self-conscious.

He stepped away from the console, leaving it to his companion. Grasping the rail of the *Fulmar*, and pulling himself along on ropes, he made his way forward. Walking was challenging moving at such a pace.

Stepping close to the balloon, he listened. During the *Fulmar's* test flights, he had attuned his ear to the sounds it made. Now, the rush of gas filling the chimney from the canister was undulating, spluttery, and the balloon canvas billowed. It was not taut. The canister was running low.

The spares were kept in the nose of the vessel, to counterbalance the engine in the rear. Balfour had become used to replacing them by himself. His companion was more content to stand by and steer, while Balfour performed the task.

He cut one of the four-foot canisters from where they were secured beneath a tarpaulin and eased it across the deck. Sliding it through the slit in the net and under the balloon, he secured the base with iron clasps. Yanking out the rubber plug, he secured the mouth of the canister to one of the vents in the steel foot of the balloon's chimney, pulling free the pin that allowed the gas to flow upwards. When the canvas of the balloon began to stretch again, he unscrewed the dwindling canister. One blast of fumes escaped from the gap, but he forced the plug from the new canister into the vent, sealing it. He listened. The roar was steady. The new canister was doing its work.

He stowed the empty with its fellows and made his way towards the trapdoor that led below. He didn't tell his companion where he was going. In such a small airship, he would have no trouble finding him if he needed him. He never had done yet.

The cabin was a tiny, cramped space, where even a short man would have to bend to walk. Hunched forward, head down. Balfour moved across the creaking boards, between the ramshackle cupboards to a rickety desk. Spread upon it were various maps and charts, and a leather-bound ledger.

Seating himself, Balfour selected a pencil. He had brought no pens, fearing ink would freeze at these temperatures. Even below deck, his breath misted before him, and when he removed his gloves to write, it only took seconds for his skin to pinken and chap. He turned to the next empty page of the ledger, with the seal of the Royal Geographical Society emblazoned across the top. He began.

19th August, 1922

Day Two of the Trans-Arctic Flight Expedition. Thirty-four hours outbound from Longyearbyen. Averaging seventeen knots. Estimated arrival in Barrow, Alaska: 20th August, late evening. Weather conditions favourable.

Balfour glanced at the barometer in its brass frame.

Barometer reading: 30.68

Just then, he became aware of a noise, like breath pushed through the teeth of a nervous man. He glanced around him.

When she was built, the weight considerations of the *Fulmar* had allowed for windows. Two portholes looked out on each side. From the edge of one of the starboard planes, a thin stream of vapour gushed into the cabin.

Investigating, Balfour found one of the bolts had come loose. He sighed. The wingnuts securing the windows were on the outside of the ship. If a crewmember lost their senses, as some might, trapped aboard a floating wooden prison, they could not unbolt the window from within and hurl themselves out.

Back on deck, Balfour called to his companion.

"Problem with the window. I'm going over to fix it."

From a sea chest in the prow, he took a harness, belting it around his waist, legs, and body. Two long ropes depended from it.

"Make these fast on the other end," he said and leaned over the starboard rail. The damage to the window was not severe, but he could see the top-left wingnut was a deal looser than the other, allowing warm air and pressure to escape from the cabin.

Balfour swung one leg over the side of the *Fulmar*. He grasped the rail, preparing to drop the other over, when he happened to glance back.

The two ropes still trailed along the deck, not tied to anything.

Alarm rose like bile in his throat as he sprang back into the ship.

"Didn't you hear me, you stupid ass?" he demanded, anger replacing his fear. "I said to tie me off! You could've sent me to my death!"

Not waiting for a reply or an apology, Balfour made the lifelines fast himself, muttering furiously. When he was satisfied the knots were tight, he returned to his work, dropping over the side of the airship. Feet braced against the hull, he manoeuvred himself to the porthole, and began tightening the wingnut.

His long fur coat billowed like broken wings. Once, he glanced down between his legs. They were over a break in the clouds, and through that could be seen the blue featurelessness of the Arctic Ocean, twenty thousand feet below him. No land, no ice. An uninterrupted plummet to bone-breaking impact with the water and a certain, freezing death.

No such thing occurred. The window was re-tightened, and Balfour hauled himself, hand over hand, back onto the deck.

"Do try and pay attention to orders," he called to his companion, as he removed the harness and stashed it. "That was very nearly the death of me."

The other was silent, ashamed, and Balfour returned below.

In the cabin, he set a kettle of water to boil on the little paraffin burner. He and his companion had rationed themselves to one cup of tea a day, although the other fellow left his untouched on the countertops. He had never complained, but he didn't seem to like tea.

Balfour, on the other hand, always drank with relish. The beverage would flow through his limbs until he was, somehow, warm again. The effect was fleeting, would pass in only minutes, but it was something in the day to look forward to; an oasis in the icy vastness of the Arctic sky where he would be warm.

Sitting at the desk, waiting for the water, his eyes fell on a book with a black cover. Silver lettering on the spine read: 'SOUTH: THE STORY OF THE 1914–1917 EXPEDITION – SIR ERNEST SHACKLETON C.VO.'

The edges of the pages were jagged and shredded from many readings, though the book itself was only three years old. Balfour laid a hand on the cover, and felt the spasm of fear he had felt in glancing down at the ocean below faded away.

The kettle hissed. Balfour prepared the tea slowly, letting the steam wash over his face. He was raising his fragrant cup to his lips when the barometer caught his eyes.

It read 28.02.

He blinked, frowned at the instrument.

No, 27.98.

It had fallen two points below standard pressure in the ten or so minutes since he had last looked at it.

The light over his face faded. He looked through the porthole he had just fixed. The air outside was darkening. He set down the teacup so hard that it cracked. He ignored it, racing to the ladder and swinging up onto the deck. The moment he was topside, a great rolling wind tumbled by, shifting his hat on his head, fanning his coat. The sky had gone from startling blue to scowling grey. The cold ripped through his furs.

Directly ahead, extending for unguessable miles across the sky, were advancing ranks of black clouds. They swirled and coiled like the smoke of a forest fire.

Even as he looked, the wind roared louder like a wounded beast, and he staggered under its force. He heard the balloon, and the sails cry out in protest. Where had it come from?

He did not have to check the charts. They were miles from land. He could not risk steering around the storm. It would be on them in moments.

"The balloon!" he bellowed into the wind, racing to the helm, which his companion left free for him. "Release the canisters! We must lose height!"

Grasping the cranks, Balfour faced the storm.

"Two points northwest!" he cried. The stormfront looked furthest away in that direction. It would buy them more time.

The sails shifted in response to the cranks. In the howling gale, the *Fulmar* pitched onto the course he set and began racing towards the storm. Balfour had to lean steeply to prevent being thrown over.

Nearer and nearer they drew. He could see the hurricanes of snow beneath the clouds, knew that if they met them head on, they would be lost in a torrent of icy blasts. Their only hope was to fall far enough below the storm that they could avoid the worst of it and wait out the snow.

With that thought, he checked the balloon.

The canvas was taut. No gas had been released. Their height had not changed.

"Are you mad?" he hollered to his companion. "We must drop! The canisters!"

There was no answer. The canisters had not been touched.

"Where are you?"

Balfour cast left and right for a sign of his companion, and the help he might lend.

There was neither hide nor hair of him.

As the battering storm swept to meet him, Balfour thought of his companion's silence. He thought of the untouched cups of tea in the cabin. And he thought of a passage from the dog-eared book on his desk, which had always sent a shiver up his spine.

"I know that during that long and racking march of thirty-six hours over the unnamed mountains and glaciers of South Georgia it seemed to me often that we were four, and not three."

It had seemed to Balfour that they had been two, and not one.

28 MILES

by Anna Jenkins

You call Big Sister: she doesn't answer.

When you leave a message, you keep your voice measured. If the worst has already happened, Big Sister will have stopped counting several days ago. It's been a while since you heard from her, and it seems unlikely that no news is good news. You remind yourself that you are not her minder but check the times since she was last active online on three social media accounts.

You prepare for work, your bitten nails bleeding once again. You dress for the occasion, something professional, but something you wouldn't mind wearing in A&E either. You consider driving to her house before work, clocking the time. Not to go in—just to look. *For what exactly? She's a grown woman, she can take care of herself.* You think of your seven-year-old niece and take out your phone again.

You call Big Sister: she doesn't answer.

You're driving through the town centre before you realise you're driving at all. The road and buses are packed. Sun hats and summer dresses skip down the road with their parents.

You can't return their smiles. Children are steered away from the traffic, and you become angry that Niece may have walked to school alone. Maybe for days. Weeks. You wonder what she had for tea. For a moment, you consider ringing Niece's school. *I'm just a bit concerned because I've seen a child in your uniform walking to school alone. She looked too young, and I really thought someone should be with her.* You think better of it, shaking your head. You're many things but you're not a grass.

By the zebra crossing, there is chatter and excitement and you half-hear something about a cake sale through the open window. You thought you would be you by now. Mummy. Not occasional aunt/sometimes legal guardian. Not a go-between for Mum who *just can't* anymore. Not exhausted officer worker waiting for another call to tell you to put your life on hold again. It ended your relationship. *No it didn't; he couldn't hack it.* You shake the idea off. *This is no one's fault; it is what it is.* You think you feel your phone vibrating in your pocket.

You were wrong.

You call Big Sister: she doesn't answer.

You have become accustomed to days punctuated by moments of panic. For the first hour, you keep your phone out on the desk in front of you. It sits between papers and two framed photographs of Niece, one taken the day she was born and another from when your spare room was hers. You periodically resurrect the screen. You try syncing your notifications to your fitness tracker; that way, there'll be an angry-wasp buzz as soon as she calls you, and your line manager might stop asking if everything's okay. You don't trust it. Finally, you put the phone under lock and key and in the grim staffroom, wishing you could do the same to Big Sister only to find yourself tearing up the stairs to retrieve it on your break. *Of course she hasn't messaged.*

You call Big Sister: she doesn't answer.

You begin to imagine her Anna-Nicole Smithing around her shabby flat. *What if she falls asleep in the bath again?* You realise how naïve you're being when you picture her holding a wine glass. You wonder when she last bothered to decant anything from a bottle into anything other than her mouth. You picture her red-wine-lipped, slurring. Niece knows to call you in an emergency, but what if Big Sister has taken the phone with her? *Would she think this was anything less than normal?*

Last time this happened, Niece became selectively mute. Months of board games, picture exchanging and art therapy finally broke through, but again? You don't think you have it in you. You remind yourself this isn't about you. *It's worth one more attempt.*

You call Big Sister: she doesn't answer.

At lunch, you decide to get ahead of the game. Pre-empting a call from Niece's social worker, you phone her and leave a message. *Can you call me back?* She never does. You feel a grim sense of relief: this must mean she's busy with families who are worse than yours. There must be mums out there doing a worse job than Big Sister. Your jaw unclenches. *What if Big Sister is just...busy? What if she's got a new job?* Just the thought begins to soothe you, until another one rears its head. *What if she's got a new fella?*

You call Big Sister: she doesn't answer.

When four o'clock rolls around, school rings to say Niece hasn't been collected. Colleagues crane necks and strain ears as you mumble down the phone. You know this isn't the first time, you don't know where Big Sister is, you're very grateful to the staff, and you know it's late. You'll come as quickly as you can. And there you go again. You make sure it looks like you have it together enough to collect a child from school, knowing full well your demeanour and dress will be noted in the report that will inevitably be filed under Niece's name. Best-case scenario: 'middle-class, well-dressed'. They might leave you all alone that way. It's odd. When a safeguarding concern is raised, every action, every word becomes suspect. You've seen phrases like 'sullen and uncooperative' jotted out of context in Big Sister's notes; the ones made on the anniversary of baby Nephew's death. No one wakes up one day and chooses to be like her.

You call Big Sister: she doesn't answer.

You run out to the car, erasing the mental 'to-do' list you wrote just in case this evening remained your own. At the lights, you scroll through your phone trying to find the number for Big Sister and Niece's key worker. You tell yourself over and over again that this is in Niece's best interests. You aren't suggesting she goes into care; you're offering to take her yourself. After all, you can't take Niece home if Big Sister has choked on her own sick and someone involved in her case should know where she's gone. You like Key Worker; she is patient and understanding. You are still amazed at how many of them aren't. Niece likes Key Worker because she wears hooped earrings and long skirts and looks a bit like Esmerelda from '*The Hunchback of Notre Dame*'. To your dismay, you find three contacts listed as Key Worker. None of them answer, anyway. The driver of the car behind you leans on the horn, gesticulating unimaginatively in your rear-view mirror.

You call Big Sister: she doesn't answer.

Your phone rings on the gridlocked motorway. Its vibrations make you jump, and it slips like a fish through your hands to the floor: it is Little Sister. Little Sister wants to call the police. She is out of patience and has no intention of being the one to tell Niece her mother has 'done a Winehouse'. Little Sister was a midwife but gave it up when she married her husband. She lives in a barn conversion with white carpets. Her cats are both named after Egyptian goddesses. Little Sister is debating whether to call Mum. You panic, imagining Mum's panic as she imagines Niece's panic, and tell her not to, if she hasn't been in contact before ten then you'll call her. Little Sister says she hasn't got the space to take Niece in again, and you try to remember a time she ever did.

The traffic limps forwards, and the shallowest part of you ages as it dawns on you Niece's school must have rung Little Sister first and she must have said no. Little Sister lives twelve miles closer. There is a physical pain as you realise Litter Sister is Niece's first emergency contact, not you, even though you have privately fostered Niece on four separate occasions in a failed attempt to keep the social at arm's length.

Little Sister's coldness has surprised you, and you begin to wonder if you're the weak one. Are you enabling this? Are you making her worse? Are you letting her get away with being a crap mum? Whilst she has one dead child, she has one live one too, and surely that's something worth fighting for? You try to remember a time when it wasn't like this. When it wasn't chaos; but when Nephew was born, you were fourteen, Big Sister barely out of school. Her borderline personality disorder had already hospitalised her twice, and all the photos of Nephew are accompanied by Big Sister's gashed wrists and forearms, Cheshire-Cat grins ghoulish against her pale skin. She wouldn't, would she? She wouldn't try that now? You panic.

You call Big Sister: she doesn't answer.

You call the school to give an ETA and ask to speak to Niece. They act like you've asked them to make a human sacrifice. After much exasperation, Niece is handed the phone. You are angry when she apologises like this is her fault. You become aware that you're strangling the steering wheel when the skin on your knuckles pulls tighter than Jocelyn Wildenstein's face. You tell her you'll be there as quickly as possible. When she asks why Auntie Little Sister isn't coming instead, you want to strangle her too. She asks if you've spoken to her mum You can't lie, so you ask her what she wants for tea. She mumbles something noncommittal and you know she's seen right through you.

You call Big Sister: she doesn't answer.

You arrive at the school, and you have to park around the corner because all the gates are locked. That's when Mum calls: shrill, hysterical and all the other terrible words assigned to women who have finally had enough.

Little Sister has called her, worried, although not worried enough to come to collect Niece herself, you recall. Your attempts to calm her down roll off like raindrops on a bouncy castle. She says she can't believe this is happening. You'd be forgiven for thinking she was talking about her alcoholic daughter who is missing, wasting her life and neglecting her grandchild too, but no. She's talking about you. She throws words like betrayal and sneaking and covering at you until you hang up on her mid-rant. Whilst you have grown accustomed to this sort of powerless attack, it doesn't sting any less. You give her one last chance.

You call Big Sister: she doesn't answer.

As you approach the door, you imagine Niece sitting at a too-small table on a too-small chair, wearing, you'll notice, too-small shoes. You'll buy her some new ones on the way home. Teacher will whisper to you in hushed tones, but she needn't bother. Niece's ears will prick, and you know she'll be full of questions on the long drive back to yours where she'll be staying for the night, the week, the month, who knows? You dread the morning, when you'll have to drive her back here and then drive back to work in rush-hour traffic and begin to count how many sick days you have left. You buzz intercoms and sign in, a facsimile of safeguarding, like they don't release Niece into the care of a walking grenade at the end of each day. Except, when you get inside, Niece is nowhere to be found. Instead, a puzzled teacher, arms full of books, tells you that Big Sister arrived some ten minutes previously and collected Niece herself, "Didn't she tell you?" No, you think, she did not. You thank her and apologise. The teacher waits for you to say something more, the pair of you jerking to life at the same time, a clumsy jig in the narrow doorway.

As you leave, you notice the birds are singing.

NEW ENDINGS

by Justine Bondare

The cashier is looking at you.

"Would you like a receipt?"

"Yes, thank you."

You think you stutter. Say it again.

"Thank you."

Take the paper bag from her hands. The touch alarms you. Try not to show it. Repeat yourself to make sure you've been polite.

"Sorry?"

She is still looking at you. Shake your head and step back. She looks at the next customer. Look into the bag. The receipt is still there.

A young girl waves her hand as you exit the store. The bells chime in your ears, and so does her voice.

"Happy New Year!"

Nod and step back onto the street. Remember to be polite.

"Thank you." The door has already slammed shut. The girl is gone.

Join the flow of people. Raincoats and umbrellas all melt into one. It will rain soon. The wind rustles the paper bag. Stop to open it. A large body crashes into you from behind.

"Hey, watch it!"

A man glares at you. He fixes his coat and turns around to keep walking. Forget to apologise. Watch him walk away. Thank the girl from the store one more time. The woman waiting at the bus stop looks at you. Remember about the bag. Look down.

The receipt is still there. Start walking again. Walk against the howling wind. Hold onto the paper bag. Hold it tight.

Take two lefts until you are on Hanford Street. Take a right at the next junction. Check the time. It's quarter to five. Take one more left. Check the sign. You are on Dale Street. Count the houses.

One. The overgrown gate.

Two. The barking of a poodle.

Three. The blue door.

Four. The broken fence.

Five. Go up the steps and reach into your pocket. Feel a crumpled-up bus ticket and a charity leaflet. Feel the outline of a pack of cigarettes in your back pocket. Ignore it for now. Grab your keys and unlock the door. Go inside and close the door.

The room is dark. The curtains are drawn. Part them to look out onto the street. It is motionless apart from the wind pushing the leaves along the sidewalk. Close them again. Walk over to the door and pull the handle. The breeze whistles through the gap. Fight the urge to count them again. Shake your head and shut the door. You are on Dale Street. You are home.

Look down and open the bag. The receipt is still there. Your knuckles are white from holding the bag. Stretch your hand in front of you. Count your fingers instead. Breathe in, breathe out. Remind yourself that you are home.

Pick another key from the keyring and walk down the narrow hallway. Feel for the keyhole in the door in front of you. Unlock it and press on it with your shoulder. Listen to it whine as it budges open.

Dust dances in the sudden breeze. Blink as you adapt to the new darkness. Wait until you see a staircase. Put your hand on the wall and make your way down. Hear the familiar ticking. The air is moist and smells of copper. Cough once.

Pull the string hanging by the end of the staircase. The room lights up. It is yellow and dim. The smell of copper is strong. The grandfather clock ticks in the shadows of the stairs. Tick, tock. It hides the silence. Crouch under the low ceiling and walk forward. Step over your laundry. Turn around and look up. Unclench your shoulders.

The door is closed. The ticking continues.

Put the bag on the table in the centre of the room. Don't look right, not yet. Ignore the quiet coming from her bed. The clock on the table ticks in sync with the grandfather clock. Let their ticking ease your mind. Tick, tock.

Empty your pockets. One bus ticket, one charity leaflet. One receipt. Hear yourself count.

"One. One. One."

The paper bag crunches as you take out its contents. Smoothen the receipt against the table. It curls again when you lift your hand. Feel the heat rush to your face. Breathe in. Look at the door.

It is still closed. Breathe out. The ticking continues.

Push the bag off the table and hear it land on a pile of others. Trace the edge of the table with your fingers. Find the familiar chip and scratch at it. Relax.

Look at the calendar you bought. The clear wrapping shines in the dim lighting. Take it in your hands. Graze your fingernail against the side. Watch as the wrapping splits. Pull at it and let it fall soundlessly to the floor.

Go to the far end of the room. Farther from the rotting. Listen to the crinkle of newspapers under your shoes. Pull another string. The nail waits on the wall. Hang the calendar next to the rest. A decade of crossed-out days. Time she will never get back.

Don't look right, not yet.

Check the time. It is two minutes to five. Close your eyes and breathe out. The ticking continues.

Wake up.

Listen to early fireworks. People shouting on the street.

Sit against the wall. It is damp against your back. The clocks have stopped. Imagine the ticking instead.

Look at the lower corner. Notice the growing mould. Watch the spores vibrating around it. Watch them crawl towards you. Cough once. Look at your hands. There's a splinter in your left thumb. Remember the chip in the wood. Tick, tock.

"Five more minutes, everyone!"

Look at the opposite corner of the basement. Make a decision.

Stand up. Feel lightheaded. Put your hand on the damp wall. Appreciate the stacks of leaflets lining the edge. Various tickets pinned to the faded wallpaper. Price tags and flyers. Let the sight calm you.

Start walking. Count your steps. Feel the smell of decomposition get closer. Smell the perfume you've tried to hide it with. Move your hand along the wall and watch the dust you push with it. Tick, tock.

Arrive at the corner.

"One minute!"

Kneel in front of the grimy mattress. Breathe in through your mouth. Hear your heartbeat pounding in your ears. Place your hands on the curled-up figure. Gently sweep the dust off her side. Smoothen her cardigan. Move away the grey hairs from her face.

"Five, four, three, two…"

Lean in and place a kiss on your mother's forehead. Ignore the smell of rot. Ignore the loud cheers above you. Lean back and place your hands on your knees.

Look behind you. Look at the door. It is closed. Check the time.

One minute past midnight.

"Happy New Year."

Wait for a response. Close your eyes and repeat yourself.

"Happy New Year." Pretend everything is all right. Pretend you can hear her voice. Check the time.

Two minutes past midnight.

Turn around and lay your head on her stomach. Look at the cobwebs on the ceiling. Remember the pack of cigarettes. Remember how much your mother loved to smoke. Reach for the pack and a lighter. Open it and take out a single cigarette. Look up as you light it.

Put the cigarette in your mouth. Inhale. Taste the familiar smell of smoke. Cough because you don't know how to smoke. Remember that she did. Try to smile.

"For you."

Put the cigarette to her mouth. Wait for her to inhale again. Wait for her stomach to move under your head. Ignore the smell of rotting flesh.

Put the cigarette on the floor and close your eyes. Pretend that everything is okay. Put your wrist to your ear. Listen to the ticking of the watch. Give her more time.

Say it again, just in case.

"Happy New Year."

Listen to the newspapers catch fire. Tick, tock.

THE BLOOD OF RAVENSCREE

by Jeni Meadows

Erik waited for her where he always did—his legs dangling over the edge of the escarpment, his feet dipping the water when the river ran high, carefully positioned behind the bushes so he couldn't be seen from the road. Tora picked her way across the scrub to meet him. She was grateful for the full moon. The wine was heavy on her thoughts, and she had to watch where she put her feet in the flatness the dark gave the landscape. As she neared, she saw Erik's chin resting on his knee, an arm wrapped around his leg. A sense of dread trickled its way in through the wine-fog.

"Couldn't you have met me at home?" she complained, dropping down next to him. The hilt of the sword strapped over her shoulder cracked her in the back of the head.

She grunted and tugged at the buckle at her throat. The sword dropped into the grass beside her. "I haven't come from home," Erik murmured, so quiet she barely heard him. He stared intently at the river flowing beneath his foot.

Tora followed his gaze while she waited for him to finish whatever thought he was in the middle of. The water was grey in the moonlight. It gurgled its happy little song beneath them, oblivious and uncaring. She tipped her head back and took a long, deep lungful of the sweet air, and as she let it out again, a fragment of the wine-fog departed with it. She mourned its passing. Beside her, Erik stirred. His foot slipped over the edge, and he took a sharp breath, as though noticing her woke him from a deep sleep. He turned to her. "How's the party?"

"It's one of his better ones," She shrugged. "Although, he's refusing to serve any mead. It's annoying a lot of people. Which I suppose was the point."

Erik smiled at this.

"I was enjoying it. What's so important you couldn't wait until morning?"

"Morning, possibly," he admitted, turning away from her to reach into a knapsack at his side. "But you don't usually emerge from Halfdan's parties until at least mid-afternoon."

She raised a mildly offended eyebrow.

Erik extracted from his bag a well-folded square of cloth and handed it to her. She looked at him hard and accepted it with a sigh.

"You dragged me all the way out here in the middle of the night for this?" Tilting the cloth into the light of the moon revealed a smudged drawing of a puzzle box, ornately carved in the ancient way, with a hole in one face the shape of a twelve-pointed star. Tora had seen this drawing too many times of late.

"It's a myth, Erik," She sighed. "How many times do I have to say it?"

"Never again, I'm sure you'll be delighted to hear."

When she looked back to him, a cloth bundle lay clutched in both hands. Tora sensed it before she saw it, before her brain had fully acknowledged the sight of it. It reached out to her with a grasping claw. She scrambled to her feet. The corner of her awareness she very much preferred to ignore latched on to the thing in Erik's hands, drawing her closer. He unwrapped the cloth, and the box within throbbed with ancient power, dripped with it, oozing it out into the air around them. Her fingers twitched. She stepped backwards, once.

"Put it away, Erik."

But he had never been one for doing what he was told. He looked up at her, eyes glinting in the moonlight, and shook his head.

"I found it," he whispered. "Everyone said it was just a legend, but I followed all the clues and hidden messages scattered throughout history, and here it is."

His words became lost to Tora. They were one layer of noise among dozens, then hundreds, of overlapping whispers, voices within the cube in a tongue she did not comprehend, growing louder and louder in her mind, drawing her towards the box. The strength of her legs failed her. She felt nothing as she hit the ground. The carvings on the box's face stood proud in the silver moon, the metalwork no man could ever dream to replicate unblemished by time and staring back at her as she tried in vain to look away.

The whispers roared in Tora's mind. One voice found her name, and the others picked it up, calling to her, taunting her, luring her towards them just as they had all those years ago. Her hands clamped over her ears, trying to block out the voices even though she knew they were inside her head. Ceaseless, screaming whispers.

"Erik..." she managed. "Please. I can't..."

She couldn't—it didn't matter. Only the whispers remained, and their relentless pull towards that box. In an instant, it was gone. Tora gasped and fell sideways onto the grass. Suddenly chilled in her own sweat, her whole body trembled. She opened her eyes with effort, and tears escaped down her cheeks.

She watched the gentle flow of the river as she calmed her breathing. For a while, all was silent. She was deaf to the sounds of the night, and she reached for them, anything to push out the echo of the whispers. The call of an owl somewhere to her left. Its mate's careless reply, further off. The grass rustling in the wind. And, eventually, the sweet bubbling of the water tripping lightly over rock and riverbed.

She gulped the air again, soothed this time by the clarity it brought to her mind. The wine-fog was long gone now.

Minutes passed in silence. She could feel Erik, watching her.

"I need you to help me." "

No."

"Please, Tora. It's real. Everyone, all the books, they said it was lost, but I found it, and I know where it can lead us. Please. The Old Magic isn't as strong for me. I can feel it, but that's not enough. It calls to you. I can see it in your face."

Tora drew her hands over her eyes. She was exhausted, suddenly.

"There's a reason why the Artefacts passed into myth," she murmured. She stared at the lights dancing in the little town across the fields, but she saw only darkness in deep caverns, far away. "The Old Gods do not want to be disturbed."

"I don't understand. An hour ago, you were regaling Lords with your valiant explorations of places unknown. Yet when I offer you the chance of riches and fame everlasting, you turn it down."

"I pilfer a few crypts of jewels no one will miss. My regaling is greatly exaggerated. I have achieved a perfect balance between what is songworthy and what won't get me killed. You are talking about stealing from the graves of Gods."

"What's the difference? There's nothing up there but dust and bones."

Tora shook her head slowly. Memories she'd tried to forget displayed themselves before her eyes. "I went up to Ravenscree once," she confessed. She didn't look to see Erik's expression. "That's where it's pointing you, isn't it? Of course it is. I was younger then, and brazen. That ruin had claimed the lives of so many, but I was determined it would not conquer me." She laughed softly. "I was a clueless fool. There is life in those stones. They watch you from the moment you set foot in the courtyard, and they follow you right to the door. Thousands of years and Nature never reclaimed that valley. I don't think She's dared to try." Tora looked Erik straight in the eye, and he flinched. "I stood on the threshold, and the Old Gods called to me. They spoke my name and they told me of all the things I feared and hoped to be true. I heard movement in that darkness, I saw things that should not be alive looking back at me. They endure there, among their dust and their bones. And you think you can take what is theirs just because you found their little toy?"

Erik looked away from her, out across the fields. "The Magic recognised one of its own," he argued. "It lingers there, perhaps, but nothing could possibly be alive."

"Don't tell me what I saw. You weren't there. I want to die old and full and surrounded by people who love me. Not to disappear to time in a cold, forbidden tomb."

Erik said nothing. He'd drawn his knee back up under his chin.

"I'm sorry, Erik," she finished, and slowly got to her feet. "I can't help you with this." She picked up her sword from the ground and pulled the strap over her head. The weight of it nestled between her shoulder blades brought her some small peace.

"I know why you're afraid," Erik said to the river.

"Oh?"

"These are things that have no right to exist in this world. You don't want to face them. I understand that. No one does. But they do exist, and they chose you to carry their power, just like they chose me to find their Key. You can feel it. I know you can, because I can feel it, and my gift is nothing to yours."

Tora closed her eyes. The puzzle box throbbed at her attention.

"It's better left alone," she insisted, quietly, to it just as much as to him. He turned to face her, his legs crossed before him.

"You have run from your power ever since you were a little girl. I think now is the time to command it."

"And I think that anything locked away inside a tomb and left to crumble for a thousand years is meant to stay there. You and I cannot battle such things, whether we have an ancient power or not."

He got up and went to her and gripped her shoulders in his hands. They weren't strong, but they meant well.

"Of course we can," he whispered, "as we always do. Me with my books, and you with that massive sword."

She did not believe him. He saw it in her face.

"Are you going up there, even if I don't?"

"No. I don't have your courage, or the Magic in your blood. I wouldn't get very far on my own." She stepped away. Her back turned towards everything they had both ever called home, and she looked up to where she knew Ravenscree Peak loomed in the darkness, waiting for her. It had always called to her. She had always known better than to answer.

"Give me a day. I will find you at nightfall tomorrow."

"Very well." Erik returned to the edge of the escarpment and graciously sank back into the grass. His leg folded back up beneath his chin. One hand rested protectively on his knapsack, the other, after a moment, traced absent patterns in the stitching of his trousers. There was much Tora felt the need to say, but their conversation had finished for him, and she knew he would not hear. She did not look back at the mountains. She returned to the road for home.

YOU JUST NEED TO BE IN THE RIGHT TIME AT THE RIGHT PLACE

by Martin Palmer

It was the quickest cigarette I've ever had. Or cigarettes. I don't know. I couldn't feel my lips, my cheeks, or even taste the smoke. I just saw myself light up, like on a grainy CCTV monitor, saw some wrapping stuck out the side of our kitchen bins flapping in the wind, saw my hand moving away from, then back up to, my face.

"Dan?" The sound reached me like the click of a kettle— though I couldn't hear the water boiling. "Come on back in, Dan. I think we're ready to talk."

Now it was all in my stomach. They call them butterflies, but it felt more like a cold mass of maggots, weighing me down and yet making me feel empty at the same time. I thought I might be sick, so I steadied myself against one of the Biffa bins. Some of the recycling had fallen out of it, a scrap of cardboard, on it the words "ALTO FRAGILE."

I looked at the whiteness of my knuckles against the blue of the bin, edges feathered by repeated scrapes. The blood, still wet between my fingers, caught the weakest of light coming through the thick clouds that had settled over the day. It was forecast for rain, I remember thinking as I went back inside. It's all we ever talk about before a big booking: *let's hope it's beer garden weather*, said over and over again until it becomes as full of meaning as a breath.

I came back in through the cellar doors. We weren't supposed to keep them open, unless for a delivery, but maybe someone forgot. The chillers in there are great, making the space icy in comparison to our kitchen. The makers obviously agree, judging by their branding—'Arctic Factor' written down the length of a cartoon icicle on the side of the unit. I read it as I washed my hands off in the grotty little sink there.

The cool air and the mustiness, mixed with sugary fruits from a dropped alcopop, brought me back round a little bit. I went through the corridor outside the cellar and opened the door to our staffroom. Mike was already there, as was Baz, head tilted back so it looked like he was trying to snort the strip light off the ceiling. Well, he might've snorted it, but his nostrils were full of bloody cotton wool. There was blood crusted around his lip, too, and down his ever-so-hip denim shirt, dribbling in a dried red river that reached his huge, blingy belt buckle.

He flinched as I walked over to him. Laura was fussing around him, and probably flicked his eyelash or something. I found myself wondering why she should care so much.

Customers like him gave everyone shit, even if just by being arrogant. And her... I'd have thought she'd know a bit of what the game was about, y'know, thought she had him made, but hey, who knows what goes on behind closed doors? Maybe I could find out by switching time again.

"Right, Laura, I don't think it's mortal, so you can get back to the bar now, thanks," said Mike. She huffed a bit, as if the moment she left Baz might keel over, but all three of us glared at her, and she got the message. "Thanks for coming in, Dan."

"I've got to be here, haven't I?"

"Well, yes, but what I mean is..." Mike shifted his weight and looked between Baz and me, hoping one of us was going to finish his sentence for him.

"It's a serious situation. I'm glad you're on the team, and that, as a team, we can resolve Baz's issue."

"How long have we got?" I let the comment hang in the air. I could still hear the chiller whirring away like an old piece of farm equipment. The smell of liberally applied Lynx stuck to the room like chewing gum under a table. Baz, of course, must have been enjoying 'subtle tones of wet metal and fluffiness' with what he had shoved up his nose.

"I want blood!" he growled.

"You've got plenty of that," I said.

I thought his eyes might actually burst from anger. Mike, like the wet blanket he was, immediately flashed Baz the most sickening grin ever. I'd been more sincere in telling my father-in-law that Liverpool probably did deserve to win the league last year. Not gonna happen, mate.

"It's a disgrace," Baz started. "Your granddaughters only get christened once! I paid for all this spread to be put on, and it wasn't. I have all these starving mouths to feed, trying to support this poxy place, and then, when I try and have a decent conversation with the staff, try and sort it out, this is what fookin' 'appens."

He made a sweeping gesture with his hand, and as he did so, one of his cotton balls fell out. I envied the ball, saying 'fuck this', and taking charge of its situation.

"Add to that the 'unsafe conditions' that have led to my..." He gestured to his nose, noticed the missing ball, and paused while he bent to pick it up. His face was red again from bending over. "I mean, I think some kind of compensation is well and fucking truly due, don't you?"

"Hey, you're a poet and you didn't know it."

"Please, Dan. Baz is making a very good point."

Mike began wringing his hands, as if trying to rid them of sweat.

"Well, here's a good point for the both of you—why was he even in the kitchen?"

I raised my eyebrows. Baz held my gaze, and I thought, that's just so typical of him. Any normal person would be ashamed at such entitled behaviour. Not him. And as for Mike, well... Any normal manager would've barred the bastard by now. But this is no normal place. This is The Duchess and Bank.

"There's a big, fuck-off 'STAFF ONLY' sign on the door."

"I practically am fucking staff, the amount I do around here," Baz said, putting his hands on his hips.

His efforts were news to me. All I ever heard him do, even from where I was, in the kitchen, was criticise and complain.

"Well, since you're a fully-fledged member of the team, you'll know that the correct procedure for spillages is to get a wet-floor sign out—which I was about to do before you came barging in. I didn't know ahead of time that there'd be a pool of gravy right where your foot was going to be, did I? If I could fucking see the future, don't you think I'd win the lottery, buy this shithole, bulldoze it with you lot in it, and move to Spain?"

"Hah-ha, that's just an expression, you understand," said Mike, scratching his nose. "I think what Dan is trying to say is that we're keen on health and safety here. It's in our make-up from top to bottom. What happened to you was, well, something of a freak accident."

He looked relieved that I had mentioned standard operating procedure. It gave him opportunity to quote the book in his awkward management-speak. Baz shook his head and tutted. He breathed out through his teeth, and I felt the air pressure in the room suddenly drop. He launched his right fist into one of our lockers, leaving a big dent. They were probably as old as the pub itself, and missing a bit of paint here and there, but had survived without major damage until now. Mike rested a hand on his chest. If I was standing where he was, I'd have put my hands up, ready to deck this wanker, but I stayed calm. I'd seen all this before, this knobhead behaviour, knew the best bet to lay.

There was a tinny clatter as a carefully placed can of deodorant fell to the floor from the top of the unit. "Wow, what a hit. Bit below the belt, but—"

"I've had enough of your fookin' smart alec-comments," Baz snarled, pointing at me, his knuckles split and showing signs of blood coming to the surface. "Don't think I don't know about what you've been saying about me and Laura behind my back. I'm married."

I held up my hands and marvelled at this oaf's impotent rage. "That's ridiculous!"

Baz raised an eyebrow, not expecting me to try and placate him.

"I think the whole team here appreciates what a loyal and upstanding customer you are." At this, Mike twisted his head to look at me and let his mouth hang open. "You're very nice to the staff," I added.

Baz smirked, always a fan of a compliment, however slimy.

"You just decided to give Laura more than your tip."

Baz's face dropped to the floor. He raised his hand again and took a step toward me. I saw what happened next on two reels—one moving quickly, the other in slow motion, and in the middle, there was reality. He stepped on the deodorant can at his feet, balance so thrown off by his lunge toward me that he didn't even wobble before falling over. He landed on Mike, rugby-tackling him to the floor in the process. I tried not to laugh out loud. I failed. It's not often I get out early on a Sunday.

The skies had brightened up a bit, and it was almost a shame to be driving, not outside in the sun. I knew the forecast would be wrong after I last switched time. I pulled up to the little corner shop on my way home. I know them by name in there. Rob and I are kindred spirits, unsung heroes in the fight against arsehole customers—you should see some of the stick he gets off the locals when he won't sell them scratch cards underage. He can tell by the nod I give him that I understand.

I plonk my usual tinnies down on the countertop, and they make a sound a bit like a chair scraping on lino. "Looking forward to these," I say, as he whips out a carrier bag from the pile hung up on the wall.

"Anything else for you, mate?" he asks, knowing there never is, holding out his hand for the exact change I normally have ready.

"Actually, yeah, go on. It's a big rollover tonight, isn't it? Fancy I'll have a go."

POETRY

WINNER

THE BEGONIA BUSH
BY KAYLA JENKINS

'This is intimate, moving surprising, full of colour and structurally full of light: the smoky evening light of youth contemplating age, with love, patience and the tender horror of the grotesqueness of aging. Sentiment is avoided here with humour and precise honesty about the central relationship, the lines are tight, and the poem surprises the reader in the end with a sense of dark hope. An emotionally fraught journey told with crisp imagery.'

– Eoghan Walls
Head Poetry Judge

THE BEGONIA BUSH

by Kayla Jenkins

My grandmother sits on the patio outside

at dusk, smoking her fourth cig of the hour.

She's a murmur now, confined to the clots

in her lungs and the empty sleeves

of my grandfather's old favourite shit-shirt.

I wonder what she listens to; perhaps

the crisp fall of begonia petals onto concrete

as the bushel begins to shed, or else

the rush of dirty water out the pipe as my mother

stands at the kitchen window, washing

the dishes. Neither will look at the other,

no raised eyes in the same shade of grey—

in a quarter of an hour my mother will poke

her head around the door, ask *would you*

like a cuppa, Mum? My grandmother will nod,

wordlessly pass her mug over as she watches

another John Wayne rerun—probably '*Rio Bravo*'

or '*Big Jake*'—not '*True Grit*', though, my grandmother

never favoured the popular ones. Taking one last drag,

she stubs out her cig and adds it to the growing pile

half-buried in the begonia soil. I'll clean it out

tomorrow, while I'm planting the new seeds

RUNNERS UP

高天原 – TAKAMAGAHARA
BY COURTENAY S. GRAY

'Part body horror, part love-letter, this haibun refuses to fully resolve one genre in the other—or perhaps, where resolution might appear, bursting out of the reader's stomach, we are introduced to a further cerebral horror—as memory and narrative sureness slip from our grasp right as the beast crawls through us. France is clashed with Japan—literary traditions and languages smashing—in crisp, disturbing images. Yes.'

EVERY OTHER FRIDAY
BY CAIT COOK

'There is an emotional and imagistic awareness to this verse that is utterly disarming. This is unsentimental, sharp, and harrowing to read: about the things we put ourselves through, with clear eyes on the harm done to the persona of the poem,

and an explorative honest attempt to think or rethink sex as a form of harm. The bare forthrightness still carries the reader with images, but is also a forceful questioning which does not resolve itself with any easy answers. A brave investigation.'

– Eoghan Walls
Head Poetry Judge

高天原 – TAKAMAGAHARA

by Courtenay S. Gray

One evening in Paris, when the air was swirling with fog and your cigar smoke, I kissed you for the first time. I rested my head on your shoulder, lashes thick with black mascara. A teardrop, Prussian Blue, dropped on your neck and I licked it off with my tongue like a serpent. I placed my hand on your stomach, swirling my fingers around gently. That's when I felt it, the movement. Your eyes widened and you began to panic. I lifted your shirt and saw what appeared to be a parasite making its way up to your ribs cruising underneath your skin. It salivates at the purity of your flesh, raw like a womb. My breath echoed yours, reaching an erratic crescendo of confusion and fear. Your eyes began to close, and your heartbeat began to slow, until it became a distant memory. Death forces you to retrace your own memory, to question your own sanity. You see, we never made it to Paris. You died before we could walk along the rivers of Paris, before I could glaze your mouth with my oral rose. The creature that stirs in the underbelly of hell is the enemy I wish I had never had to endure.

The graveyard of bones—
Thrives on the creature in you—
Oozing black treacle

EVERY OTHER FRIDAY

by Cait Cook

I've gotten high to write this, to feel less as I do.
So when my clichés unfurl as I think what sex should be,
it's because I am within one.

But they don't. Nothing unfurls.
There are no red lights or melting bodies, shadows tracing
the hook of a spine.
The bar died far below.

I just don't want to be polite.

To let you inside through courtesy.
Moaning in a way that doesn't sound like pain when
it hurts
as you drive through me.

I agree and I want it but then I'm
aching on all fours. Making sounds to soften
slaps as I push back, my hair in your hand
a leash, to aid your violent depth.

It is the threat of destroying your good time,
which I am chosen as the vessel of.
Unable to ask you please
get out of me now.

When we cuddle post your climax, I am placed to hold
your side.
My excuses wait politely till they show you out the door,
till I can be alone, to wonder why I'm here again.

Curl up round a pillow, ring someone who loves me,
say it wasn't very nice,
that the pit of my stomach is sore.

They wish that I could have good sex,
as if that were the point.
That it isn't my submission to hands staining my skin which
calls for their concern.
But I say I wish the same, still knowing
the next horrendous many years will be defined by
shame, pain, the space hollowed inside me.

Yet I still hope as my nails tear the sheets, it may turn into
something divine.
So I will continue to mind my manners,
the next time I am broken into.

TIMPERLEY POSTAL OPTIONS

by Max Gorse

Two postboxes stand side by side, proud pillars of the village.
Majestic twins of circulation, a local postcard image.

I heard about a school of thought concerning how
you choose,
that the box you pick to house your post reflects the hand
you use.

Left-handers are inclined to feel that postbox east is best,
while right-handers with things to send are drawn to
postbox west.

I settle on a nearby bench with a flask and an Eccles cake,
to determine whether handedness relates to the course
you take.

A chap with a slick side parting comes, a letter in his
blazer breast.
He plucks it out with spindly right and slots it into
postbox west.

A spry old lady scuttles up, a card held against her chest.
She grips it tight in wizened right and tucks it into
postbox west.

A knackered busker ambles through, with a packet he's
just addressed.
He clutches it in calloused right and drops it into
postbox west.

A little girl comes running by, with an envelope stained
and creased.
She reaches high with tiny left and flings it into
postbox east.

At half past five, a van pulls up, it's the postman in his
high-vis vest.
With jaded right he turns the key and empties out
postbox west.

But after this, he drives away, and I'm shocked, to say
the least.
I stand and shout into the road: oi, aren't you doing
postbox east?

Just then, I see another van, and another postman comes.
He opens postbox east with left, and extends me two
raised thumbs.

PARALLEL UNIVERSE

by Toby Hudson

I feel something real,

or maybe I don't I'm not sure

There is only the silence,

the looping state of nothing

The endless beat

And then I feel strange again

But I could be a journalist, and go to Korea

Or write a television show, and win an award

Or I could die at twenty-three from a brain aneurysm

And I would never know

What I was here for

And maybe my daughter

Becomes another nothing

As I live out the remaining time

Inside my own head

Paths change direction in the low lights

My pupils dilate

And my presence is felt

In nothing but the sink, and the bowls, and the forks

I reuse again and again

Double vision

Or maybe I'm tired I can't explain it to them,

But it moves inwards, burrowing deeper

And my forward progress halts

As I start spinning away

Glued to a spot on the ground

It is falling out of me

And I see the endless pit, where the IV drip waits

Do I love you?

Or are you all there is

Do you think about me?

Will you come to my funeral?

In the parallel universe, the one I know I shouldn't visit

We dance together

And study readouts, but not my own

We hold each other

It all makes sense there

And my eyes are the same size

THE SOUND OF REVOLUTION

by Asad Naqvi

They rattle their chains
And it sounds a lot like freedom.
They stamp their feet and they lift their heads
And it is as if the ground quakes beneath them
Unable to bear the weight of a people
With the world
On their shoulders.

They rattle their chains
And it sounds a lot like freedom.

As the bird beats its wings against the cage that cannot hold it,
As the river overflows the bank that cannot hold it,
As the ember burns the hand that cannot hold it,
So, the people rattle the chains
That cannot hold them.

And the rhythm of this rattling is the chorus of a movement,
The stamping of their feet
The beat of liberty,
And though their mouths do not open,
They sing a song of redemption.

The singing is echoed through
The valleys of the savage land,
And weaves itself between
The fields of rope and cotton,
It can be heard above
The machinery of the factories,
It can be heard among
The cries of the city.
And there is more still to be sung.

It was a hum,
Then a song of sorrow,
It was a hymn,
And now a chant for the tomorrows
We have lost but will not mourn.
For our voices are sure
Though our chains are heavy,

They are few,
And we are many.

We will rattle our chains
Until the sound is one of absolution.

ELEGY FOR FAITH

by Rachana Hegde

Would you recognise God if he took your hand?
Or would you turn your face to the sunlight
and call it mercy. You see the ocean and
you don't even want to drown anymore.
But the thought is there and later
it ripples through your ghost.

The rain is striking you tonight,
burying itself in your skin. Moonlight
like a net of gauze cast at sea.
The photo on your phone shows
your face receding into grains of sand,
waves carving the beach.

You should be honest with yourself.
Think: how hard it is to want to live.
Nothing is guaranteed in the lake of your mind,
a single note can ring for hours, carried
throughout you. Compulsion touches
the heart of you with cool, eager fingers.

And when it rains inside you, the dirt
surrounding your lake is drenched.
Oh, it yearns to be found,
something sleepless and lonely.

You who would follow God
into a sky thickening with stars.
Do you remember when he let go?
How you mourned the death
of your faint bells pealing away
the pearled hours of daylight.

Some part of you will die
to make way for fresh growth,
your soil damp and ready.

And God will be there still
as the moon resting
in a bank of clouds

TO MY DEAREST Z

by Yara Stepurova

Ocher scuffed travel bag
was a mythical animal
living under your bed
for years
you fed it in secrecy
with postcard, brochures,
librettos and letters:

a choir concert,
some international fair
honouring technical progress,
square sticker from a travel bureau
with what looks like St. Basil's
in mauve and copper then—

ten letters turned one
with a green money strap;
he asks you to marry him
in the penultimate, but I know
you have never said yes
to him or to anyone,

and I can't help but wonder
why haven't you,
looking around the soviet flat,
empty with people, full of memorabilia.
Even after your Jewish mother died.

After all, you had numbered them,
the letters. They were
the only orderly unit I saw,
unclasping the jaws
of your life numb keeper.

ACKNOWLEDGEMENTS

We would like to thank the following organisations and societies for aiding The Literary Lancashire Award from 2018 and beyond:

Lancaster University English Literature and Creative Writing Department

Lancaster University Project Management Society

Lancaster University Writing Society

SCAN Lancaster University

Cake Magazine

Flash Literary Journal

Bailrigg FM

BBC Radio Lancashire

Chorley Library

And, of course, our team of student and staff judges, who have massively contributed to this project and whose help is always greatly appreciated.

Sam Cardy
Charlie Fabre
Sam Reeve
Jodie Reeve

Jake Street
Ava McMeeking
Eogham Walls
Zoe Lambert

BEATEN TRACK PUBLISHING

For more titles from Beaten Track Publishing,
please visit our website:

https://www.beatentrackpublishing.com

Thanks for reading!

www.ingramcontent.com/pod-product-compliance
Lightning Source LLC
Chambersburg PA
CBHW011425200626
46814CB00017B/3010